DANIEL
in the lions' den

Written by Anne Gill
Illustrated by Kathleen McDougall

BridgeWater Books

Long ago, in the land of Babylon, there was a king named Darius. Darius's chief minister was a very wise and honest man named Daniel. Daniel helped Darius rule over the people and made sure that everyone paid their taxes.

But many people didn't like Daniel because he was a Jew from a foreign land, and they were jealous of his power. They tried to find reasons for King Darius to send Daniel away, but the King refused. Finally, the people realized the only way to get rid of Daniel was to make trouble for him through his love of God.

The leaders of the people went to King Darius and told him that there should be a law to stop anyone from praying to any god except the King. Anyone who broke the law should be cast into a den of lions. The King thought this was a good idea and agreed to sign the law.

The leaders of the people knew that Daniel prayed to God three times a day. So they followed Daniel to his home and heard him praying by an open window. They hurried to tell the King that Daniel had broken the new law and demanded that he be arrested and thrown into the lions' den.

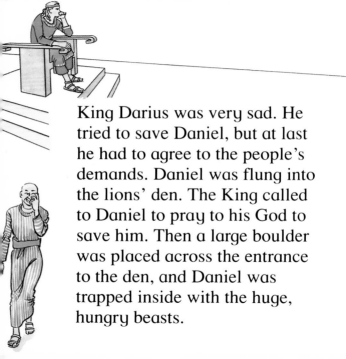

King Darius was very sad. He tried to save Daniel, but at last he had to agree to the people's demands. Daniel was flung into the lions' den. The King called to Daniel to pray to his God to save him. Then a large boulder was placed across the entrance to the den, and Daniel was trapped inside with the huge, hungry beasts.

The King didn't sleep that night. Early the next morning he rushed to the lions' den, calling Daniel's name. He was very pleased to hear Daniel's voice. Daniel told him that the lions had not harmed him because his God had protected him. The boulder was rolled back, and Daniel was pulled out unharmed.

Then King Darius called for all Daniel's enemies to be brought to him. He ordered that they and all their families be punished by being thrown into the lions' den. There the same lions who had not touched Daniel leaped on them and tore them to pieces.

King Darius then told the people
of Babylon and all the people of
the world that they should fear
Daniel's God. "He saved Daniel
from the lions and is a living
God who will rule forever."